Strange New Powers

The Black Circle Chronicles – Book 2

GARY LEE VINCENT

Strange New Powers
By **Gary Lee Vincent**

Burning Bulb Publishing
P.O. Box 4721
Bridgeport, WV 26330-4721
United States of America
www.BurningBulbPublishing.com

Cover concept by Gary Lee Vincent with photos from Idutko from Shutterstock, B-D-S Piotr Marcinski from Shutterstock, Maksim Toome from Shutterstock, and Serhii Volyk from Pexels.

First Edition.

Paperback Edition ISBN: 978-1-948278-36-2

Printed in the United States of America

DEDICATION

To my band of misfits at Burning Bulb Publishing,
who are blind to the impossible, impervious to the
opinions of the naysayers, and continuously strive to
bring exciting stories to life.
I love you all.

CHAPTER 1

Sometimes when Wendy Wilson stared out from her living room window at the perfectly manicured front lawn of her Wickenburg, Arizona home, she felt intense pleasure at the sight of the flowerbeds, with their lovely spring blossoms.

Unfortunately, this morning wasn't one of such pleasant times.

He's done it again, Wendy thought disconsolately, blinking away tears. *Mark has found himself yet another dirty woman.* Then the tears flowed in a rush from her eyes.

Wendy had been living with Mark's infidelities for five years now. His cheating on her followed a pattern. It was an intermittent happening. They would be okay for a few months with Mark acting quite loving and caring towards her (and with her hoping and praying that he'd gotten over his 'seven-year itch' or whatever it was that kept driving him into other women's arms) and then before she knew it, she'd begin finding all the evidence again; little tokens in his pocket (like matchboxes from his visits to nightclubs and motels), his sudden need to work late, and meetings outside of town that ran over the weekend.

Most times Wendy managed to convince herself that she was merely being clingy and that nothing bad was going on; she always tried to reassure herself that

Mark really was busy and was honoring their wedding vows and staying faithful to her.

But this morning? No doubt about it now. Thirty minutes ago, while putting Mark's clothes into the washing machine, Wendy had found irrefutable evidence of his latest affair: a large red smear of lipstick on the collar of one of his white shirts. Unable to continue doing the laundry, she'd come out to the living room and wandered over to the window to stare out at the lawn and the world beyond.

A sky-blue Ford pickup rolled past. That was Wendy and Mark's next door neighbor, old Timothy Lowe, the handyman/gardener at the Wickenburg branch of the Joy of Life church down the road. Timothy lived with his daughter Becky, a friendly, if rather withdrawn, schoolteacher.

For a moment Wendy wondered if maybe Becky Lowe was her husband's new mistress. But she quickly dismissed the idea: Becky Lowe was too timid to play the role of seductress.

But we're Christian's, aren't we? We're both born-again believers. We got married in church and . . . How the hell does my husband keep treating me like dirt while God just watches and does nothing to stop him?

Wendy had no answers to this question, one which she'd been asking herself for the past five years, ever since Mark's infidelities had started. They'd been a trickle at first, but that had quickly degenerated into a stream of 'strange women.' And Wendy had just kept mum about it all. All she could see to do as a Christian was to keep praying for God's intervention in their situation.

But God doesn't seem to care, does he? Year after year after year, this man keeps breaking my heart, and God—my heavenly Father—does nothing at all!

Wendy had no idea how God Almighty could look down on her intense emotional heartache and do nothing.

She left the window and walked back to one of the living room couches to sit down. The house was large—Mark was very successful—but empty, since they'd never had children.

Wendy Wilson was thirty-eight years old, a small blonde woman. Her husband Mark was forty-one, dark-haired and much larger than she was. They had been married for ten years now. Wendy had originally been employed as a waitress at Cowboy Cookin' over on Route 60, but she'd quit a few years ago. With her husband's income from his job as hedge fund manager at Wiltman Financial, the job wasn't paying her enough to justify itself—it had become more of a social outlet for Wendy than anything else.

But now, Wendy wished she still had that social outlet. Then at least, she would have something to occupy herself with other than thoughts of her husband's cheating. Now, as expected, most of her social life revolved around her church, the Joy of Life Bible Church situated down the road, but her current problems seemed more than the church (and God too) could handle for her. She had reported Mark's philandering to Pastor Fisher, and he'd counselled both of them. And each time, Mark had seemed genuinely repentant for his sins and for hurting her. But it was just for a while; give him a few months and he'd relapse again.

Wendy was sick and tired of it all. *And I've been enabling him by being so passive. Committing adultery isn't a sickness like cancer. It's a sin against your spouse caused by a lack of commitment and self-control; not to mention moral fiber!*

"But this is it!" she told herself grimly. "I've warned Mark about this before. I told him I wouldn't let him step on me like this forever . . . Indeed, if it wasn't for God and the fact that Christians aren't supposed to get divorced I'd have left him three years ago . . ."

But now, Wendy had really had enough. After finding that lipstick smear on Mark's shirt, she'd investigated it thoroughly, wondering if she'd maybe been the one who'd made it. But she'd concluded that she hadn't. For one thing, she didn't have that orange-like shade of lipstick in the house; and for another, she couldn't remember the last time she'd been held intimately enough by her husband to afford her lips an opportunity to brush his chest.

"Mark, if you're cheating on me again, this time *I will* divorce you."

She got up again, intending to head back to finish loading up the laundry into the washer. After just a few steps, however, she found herself once again drawn to the living room window that overlooked her front lawn. What had arrested her attention was the sound of a car pulling into the opposite driveway.

Almost as if a force was compelling her, Wendy walked over to the window and stared out again.

Oh, it's Karen. She watched her new neighbor Karen Houston getting out of her brother's Ford Mustang, and then opening up the car's back door and picking up several bulging grocery bags from Safeway. Once she had the bags, Karen stood in place for a moment and looked around the neighborhood.

Watching her, Wendy felt a sudden chill. To her mind, Karen Houston was a strange woman, with that flowing black hair and those blue eyes and the long dark dresses she insisted on wearing even on days as warm as this one. Wendy had spoken to Karen a few times since she and her brother had moved in opposite them, and while Karen had seemed a very amiable person, Wendy had also sensed a strangeness about her; a coldness that lay below her surface, and also something dark and dirty.

She needs God and the church. She needs Jesus, Wendy had thought then, but something forbidding about Karen had prevented her from preaching to her.

And now? Well, Wendy didn't feel like preaching to Karen now either; but she needed someone to talk. And, besides, she was overdue to invite her new neighbor over for coffee. So what better time than now?

She checked her watch. It was now 11 a.m. *So, later today, when Karen has had time to unpack her shopping purchases and maybe even take a nap too if she wants to, I'll go ring her doorbell and invite her over for coffee. Hey, but what if she's the one that Mark is having an affair with?*

5

She quickly killed that idea. Though Karen was single, she always dressed 'dark,' and the few times that Wendy had seen her wearing lipstick it had been black, not red.

CHAPTER 2

"Oh, hello. Nice to see you again," Karen Houston said on opening her front door. Karen had on her usual 'full-black' getup of long dress and a choker color reminiscent of urban-goth attire.

Wendy smiled back. She'd been uncertain of how she'd be received. It was now two in the afternoon and though she knew that Karen worked from, she'd had no way of knowing if she was free right now as they never exchanged numbers.

"I was just wondering if you'd like to come over for a cup of coffee," she told the black-haired woman.

Karen looked up at the sky, then she looked past Wendy, out at the road. "Yeah, sure, why not? I was trying to work, but I'm not getting anything done." Then she seemed to think a little. "Hey, but instead of going to your place, why don't I make coffee here for both of us." And then, before Wendy could protest, Karen stepped back from her door and pulled it wide open. "Please, come inside."

Feeling as if she had no choice but to accept the offer, Wendy stepped across the threshold. Entering the house felt really strange to her. She and Mark had been good friends with Jim Barnes, the house's previous owner, until Jim and his wife had moved up north to Flagstaff. Wendy been here many times when the Barneses lived here, and the house had had a warm and welcoming ambience to it. Jim and Angela had also been active members of the Joy of Life church.

But now . . . this same building seemed to house a darkness within. And the darkness seemed to radiate from Wendy's female companion.

It's as if Light moved out of here and Darkness moved in, Wendy thought.

As a born-again Christian, Wendy felt she could sense the presence of demonic forces in this house now. And walking into Karen Houston's living room, she was even more convinced that this place had become a stronghold of evil forces.

There were two pentagrams in evidence, both embroidered in black on red throw pillows; and all of the décor had a spooky vibe to it, like Halloween had come early. There were several paintings on the wall, all of which had the same unpleasantness to them and one of the five or six books in evidence had a cross on its front cover, which—judging from the position of the book's spine—was upside-down. In addition, the living room also contained a large number of statuettes and sculptures, all of which pointed to their owner being involved in demon worship of some kind.

She's a Satanist, Wendy thought in alarm. *She worships the Devil. I should get out of here right now.*

But Karen was already gesturing to a plush armchair, and Wendy felt that in the interest of a good neighborly relationship, she had no choice but to sit and play nice, and at least see this visit through. It was Wendy's idea after all to pay her neighbor a visit.

"I'll make the coffee; I won't be a minute," Karen said and vanished into her kitchen.

Wendy was left with her unease and her thoughts. It seemed to her that her day couldn't get worse: first she'd realized that her husband was having yet another affair, and now, her new neighbor worshipped the Devil? The house also had a strange smell to it, like the odor of burnt incense.

As promised, Karen soon returned with a tray of coffee and cookies. After serving Wendy a mug of coffee, she sat on the couch to the right of Wendy's armchair.

"S-so-so how are you finding Wickenburg?" Wendy asked. "I'm, sorry I don't recall where you and Bill said you were from originally. Or did I mix it all up and you've always lived here?"

Karen shook her head. "No, we moved here from Tucson." She sipped her coffee, nibbled a cookie and went on: "Bill simply wanted a change of change of scene. He's like that . . . while me? I'm not sure how long I'll reside here." She laughed. "Most likely until my brother finds a new girlfriend who doesn't like having me around. Then I'll move back to our home in Tucson."

Wendy nodded. Now that they were having a conversation, most of her earlier reservations about being here had subsided. She still did feel creeped out looking at the book with the upside-down cross on the cover and the throw pillows with the pentagrams on them, but she could shrug off the sense of misgiving these evoked in her.

She's a nice girl who's just going the wrong way, Wendy decided concerning the occult paraphernalia on display in the Houston sibling's residence. *I think I'll invite her to church.*

"I think the town's nice," Karen said, in reply to her earlier question. "It's a real change of pace from Tucson. For one thing, I haven't seen any addicts on the streets since our arrival here. And of course it's much quieter too. Big city life is just so noisy. In a big city, there's always background noise of one sort or another. And of course, the social scene isn't at all the same. For instance, there hardly seem to be any nightclubs here. So what do you townsfolk do for entertainment?"

"Church," Wendy said after taking a sip of her coffee.

"Huh?" Karen asked as if surprised. "Did you say *church?*"

Wendy nodded eagerly. "Yeah, sure. Mark and I are both born-again Christians. So for us the church is the center of our social life." Then she shrugged. "Hey, looking around here I can tell that you're into spiritual things too." Though Karen was still smiling, Wendy was certain that her sapphire eyes had just gotten several shades darker. Which was of course impossible.

"Hey, I don't want to holy-roll you," she went on, but . . . you never know . . . some evening when things seem a little dull you should come give our church a try. It's the Joy of Life church down the road."

What happened next was certainly a hallucination. Wendy was sure of this. One moment Karen was laughing and saying, "Yeah, cool. Maybe some night when I'm not in the mood for magic, I'll give your church a try out instead," and the next moment, Karen wasn't there on the couch at all, her place abruptly taken up by a giant black bird with huge red eyes like flaming coals and a nauseating stench like burnt rubber.

Oh, my dear Jesus! Wendy thought, too surprised to say anything. The bird was staring at her in rage and flapping its wings on the couch as if it was about to leap over the coffee table at her, and Wendy was certain that she was daydreaming. But then, just when it occurred to Wendy to call on God for help, the strange vision dissipated and Karen was once more sitting on the couch and leaning forward for a cookie.

What was that? Wendy thought. *What just happened in here? I don't—*

"Hey, that reminds me of something I wanna ask you about," Karen said suddenly, interrupting Wendy's train of thought. Then, as if noticing the look on her guest's face, she asked. "Hey, are you okay? You look really flustered now—like you just saw a ghost . . . or the Devil even."

Wendy shook her head. "No . . . no . . . it's just . . ." she left it there. She wasn't about telling Karen what she'd just hallucinated. Karen would think she was crazy. *Hell, she most likely thinks most of we born-again Christians are nutty anyway*. So it would clearly be best to deflect the conversation elsewhere. And thankfully, Karen had already provided an alternate topic for them to chat about: "Hey, what was that you were just saying . . . about you having something you wanted to ask me?"

Karen thought for a moment and then grinned. "Oh, that. It's concerning the churches here in Wickenburg. I don't know if you've noticed—no, that's silly of me. You live here and you attend church yourself, so of course you'd have noticed it . . ."

"Noticed what?"

Karen shrugged. "Well, since arriving here, I've been looking around—I've an interest in old gothic buildings—and it's strange to me that almost all of the churches here in Wickenburg are empty." She gestured to a gruesome painting of a skull on her wall. "I mean, like the churches all seem *dead*. They either have 'For Sale' signs on them, or their windows are all boarded up and you can tell no one's worshipped in the building for ages—years even."

***

Wendy sighed deeply at Karen's question. What her companion had just mentioned was the symptom of a strange puzzle that Wendy hadn't yet been able to figure out. All the churches in Wickenburg —both large and small, 'old fashioned' and Pentecostal— seemed ill-fated. One by one, over the past four years, the churches in town had been shutting down. The first to go had been an old Presbyterian place on the other side of town, then a Catholic church had shut down; which was something Wendy considered unprecedented: she'd never before heard of a Catholic church shutting down. But then it had gotten even stranger: Wendy and Mark had heard through a mutual Catholic friend that instead of the displaced parishioners motoring to a nearby town to attend mass or even switching to another denomination to worship, most of them seemed to have given up Christianity for good.

Several theories had been advanced for the churches' folding, but most people Wendy had spoken to believed the problem was merely a reflection of the 'End Times' as predicted in the scriptures. "The scriptures speak of a falling away in the last days," Pastor Fisher had preached. "And I believe that we're in the midst of that right now. Remember that our Lord Jesus himself asked: 'Nevertheless when the Son of man cometh, shall he find faith on the earth?' "

The church collapse had proceeded like dominos falling. Or like a spiritual infection that moved from denomination to denomination and leeched believers of their faith in God.

At the start, there had been eighteen churches in Wickenburg, and then there were twelve, then suddenly just seven, then only three . . . Until now there was just the Joy of Life Bible Church left. And with the kind of financial problems the Joy of Life church kept having, it was a wonder it too was still standing.

***

Karen frowned on hearing Wendy's explanation. "Wow, you don't say."

"You seem shocked," Wendy said. "Why is that?"

Karen shrugged and seemed to smile just a little. "I don't know for sure. But from what I can tell—Christianity seems to be flourishing everywhere else in America, while paganism—if you wanna call it that—is, if not exactly on the decline, well, it's taking a backseat to Christianity."

Wendy doubted that Karen, whose spiritual interests clearly leaned towards the dark side, was particularly bothered by a waning state of Christianity here in Wickenburg.

"I'd have thought you'd be pleased with the state of things here," she told Karen. "After all, isn't that what"—she gestured at the occult paraphernalia in the living room—"witchcraft is supposed to be all about?"

Karen smiled coldly. "Well, to be honest with you, my brother and do thoroughly dislike Christianity, and we're both delighted that it's becoming extinct here. We're curious as to what's causing said decline."

"But why?" Wendy asked.

Karen laughed now, an ugly and mocking sound. "Well, mainly because if we understood what's extinguishing the Christian flame here, we could easily apply the same principles across the rest of the country."

Wendy gulped, but then Karen laughed again. "Oh no, please don't take me seriously—I'm just kidding. More coffee?"

Wendy found herself nodding, even though the aura of impurity in Karen's living room had been steadily increasing for a while and had now become quite oppressive. But even though Wendy did realize that there was a whole lot in this room that the Lord Jesus Christ would definitely disapprove of, she nonetheless found herself remaining where she was and accepting a second and then a third cup of coffee from Karen Houston, and soon they were talking like old friends, even though to Wendy herself there did seem something a little unnatural about the way her liking of Karen seemed to increase by the minute.

Finally Wendy picked up a small leaflet from the coffee table, one with a completely black cover and gray lettering. "The Black Circle?" she asked. "What's this about?"

Karen explained. "Oh, the Black Circle is an anti-Christian organization that I belong to . . ."

CHAPTER 3

I think our neighbor opposite is ripe for the picking," Karen informed her brother Bill that night as the two of them sat in their living room, watching the Wilsons' residence through their open front windows.

Bill Houston, a grim-faced and tattooed man, nodded then took a sip of his chilled beer. "You think so?" he asked in a gruff voice.

Karen shrugged and put down the book of occult spells she'd been reading. "Yeah, her psychic vibe of deep unhappiness just keeps increasing. Her husband's unfaithfulness over the years is driving her nuts; she's at her wits end as to what to do. But for the church's attitude on divorce, she'd clearly have left him ages ago."

"No kids, yeah?"

"None. It's merely her love for him and her conscience still keeping them together."

Bill put down his emptied beer bottle, then he gave his younger sister a cold smile. "And we're about to completely shatter Wendy's love for her man now, ain't we?"

Karen nodded and then broke into a laugh, her long black hair flowing about her shoulders. "We most certainly are. And once she's broken and pliable and subject to our will . . . I discussed the Black Circle with her."

"What was her reaction?"

"Oh, the expected." Karen flung her hands up and pretended to be horrified. " 'Oh, no I'll never do that! I'm a born-again Christian. I can't fool around with magic . . . and you shouldn't either, Karen. That's the Devil's stuff and God frowns on such. . . . You'll go to Hell if you mess with witchcraft." Karen dropped her hands back into her lap and burst into loud laughter. "But under her protests I could see that she was really, really interested in buying what I was selling. It'll just take a little time."

"And a little pushing," her brother added. "And we're gonna help poor miserable Wendy Wilson along, ain't we?"

Karen nodded with great enthusiasm.

Bill laughed. "And then, once she's in the loop, we'll move against the Joy of Life church. It will fall like all the other churches in this town have. And soon, very soon too."

Karen smiled her deep agreement with her brother's words.

***

Now both in their thirties, Bill and Karen Houston had been members of the Black Circle since their early twenties. The Black Circle had one aim: to eradicate Christianity from America and afterwards from the entire planet.

Bill had always been an atheist anyway. During his teenaged years, he'd been content with merely a passive opposition to organized religion and drunken bar debates; but then a friend who had recognized Bill Houston's latent potential as a spiritual anarchist had introduced him to Satanism and the Black Circle organization.

Bill did have an organizational gift. He could get things arranged when no one else could; could thread a path through the most convoluted maze if need be. And he soon proved himself invaluable to the Black Circle organization.

From the time she was a little girl, Karen Houston had been attracted to the dark side of life. In high school she had naturally gravitated into Goth circles—she'd become one of the kids who dressed 'dark and creepy' and who liked art, music and movies filled with dark themes. Karen no longer remembered when she'd become a full-fledged witch. For her, it had seemed a natural progression, from high school Goth-girl who officiated at the occasional drunken séance with her friends, to performing cold-sober séances and casting malicious spells on her college sorority sisters. She'd studied Psychology as a major back then, until suddenly witchcraft was her life and she was unable to remember a past without that essential component.

For her, as for most Satanists, Christianity was an evil thing, a flawed and odious system of belief which sought to repress the natural human instincts and to prevent man's evolution to higher planes of being.

Karen had quickly followed Bill into the Black Circle Organization and had taken to it like a fish to water. Though young when they'd joined, with her magic savvy and his planning ability, their rise in the organization had been swift and soon they were planning and executing their own campaigns against the Christian church, with little or no supervision from the Black Circle overseers.

For the Houston siblings the destruction of Christianity (including as much embarrassment of Christians as was possible) was a full-time job. The Black Circle funded them and they traveled from town to town wreaking havoc on the unsuspecting followers of Jesus. They had had many successes, but several failures too—Christians couldn't always be deceived and tempted and destroyed.

And now Bill and Karen Houston were here in the little town of Wickenburg, where in the past four years, the Black Circle had destroyed the pastors and discouraged the congregations of eight Christian churches; all of which had been successfully closed to business. And Bill and Karen had been tasked, by the highest authorities of the Black Circle, with destroying the Joy of Life Bible Church in this town also. This last little church had so far proved resistant to the organization's most determined efforts to get rid of it.

Part of the problem was the fact that this little church they were currently targeting had a very active prayer group; intercessors always posed problems for satanic attacks—they were like a firewall around the members.

But the Black Circle had pulled other Christian walls down before and weren't discouraged.

There was a reason why the Black Circle wanted the town of Wickenburg devoid of churches and if possible of Christians too (though this latter seemed a tall order to the siblings, who weren't actually adverse to murder, but knew couldn't kill a large percentage of a town's population without the law asking questions), but Bill and Karen didn't know what that reason was.

But not knowing 'the reason why' didn't matter: If their bosses, the Black Circle, wanted all the churches in this town gone, then so be it. Bill and Karen were determined to do their utmost best to ensure that that was soon the case.

And the first stage of their assault on the Joy of Life Bible Church was to seek out weak, frustrated, and discouraged church members and recruit them into the Black Circle.

***

"Has he begun sleeping with her yet?" Karen asked Bill.

Bill shook his head in some anger. "Not yet. They had drinks together at La Cabana saloon on the other side of town, and then rented a room in a motel, but then he got a phone call from his wife and she became too nervous to go through with it. So they spent the time merely talking and then he drove her home again."

Karen frowned too. "We really need to speed things up. We can't wait forever for the two of them to decide they want to have sex."

The couple that Bill and Karen were discussing were Wendy Wilson's husband Mark and Becky

Lowe, the young schoolteacher who lived in the building adjacent to the Wilsons', on their right if viewed from the Houston's bungalow.

Becky was a quiet and timid woman who, even though not a Christian, wasn't a seductress either. So Karen had had to help her along, magically planting suggestive thoughts into Becky Lowe's mind, thoughts that Wendy's husband was secretly in love with her. Karen had also 'shown' Becky vivid mental scenarios in which the pair of them were a happy couple.

Becky Lowe was very lonely, something Karen had noticed the first time she'd spoken to her. She was thus very easy prey for Karen's plans.

Karen and Bill had put their plan into effect a week ago.

Becky would have no explanation for the romantic interest in her male neighbor that she'd suddenly developed. Her lust for Mark would seem completely natural to her.

Wendy's husband Mark had of course been much easier to influence into committing adultery. As the man was already used to straying from his wife's side, all that Karen had had to do was seed a few tantalizing thoughts of Becky naked in his mind; and then he'd begun salivating over his young neighbor, neglecting his wife, and making plans to cheat again.

And after that, Karen had let nature take its course. And it had—the pair had quickly become friendlier than they should be, with several clandestine nighttime rendezvous and lots of kissing already passing between them.

So yes, one thing had led to another, but not fast enough. By now they were expected to be passionate lovers, sleeping together at the slightest opportunity. But they weren't.

Karen blamed the church down the road for this. Or possibly Wendy had realized her prayers had some value.

"Things are moving much too slowly," Bill said as if reading her mind.

"I agree," Karen said, getting to her feet. "At this rate we'll be unable to move against the Joy of Life church for a month."

"What can . . . where are you going?"

Karen turned at the hallway entrance and smiled back at him, her smile that of a cat playing with a mouse. "I wanna get a few things from my room. I think it's time we upped the desperation and seduction between Mark and Becky."

Bill nodded, got up himself and walked into the kitchen to fetch himself another beer.

Karen was back a few minutes later carrying a black bag. After clearing the books off of the top of the coffee table, she unpacked the contents of her bag onto it. Those contents were a pair of wooden dolls, a black stone statue of a bird, and a roll of red cloth.

"Hmmm, this looks interesting," her brother said.

She nodded, but didn't otherwise reply him. Instead she unrolled the red cloth on top of the coffee table, moving the dolls and bird statue to the floor to permit her to do so. Spread out like this, the cloth was circular in shape and had clearly also been tailored so that it was an exact fit for the top of the coffee table.

Stitched into the red fabric was a large five-pointed star, so that now the tabletop represented a pentagram.

While Bill sipped his beer and grimly watched proceedings, Karen picked up the two dolls and the bird carving from the floor and returned them to the top of the coffee table. She placed the dolls side by side, then got out a small box from her bag, opened it up and sprinkled part of its content of black powder on the dolls.

After a look at Bill which instructed him to keep quiet, Karen began intoning softly:

"By the powers of Hell invested in me, I call on the fires of Hell to ignite the flames of lust between Mark Wilson and Becky Lowe . . ."

As her voice deepened to a guttural chant, the air over the coffee table turned misty. And then, suddenly the air over the coffee table burst into flames. The flames burnt for two or three seconds and then were sucked down into the bodies of the two dolls, which then both got up, hugged each other and then collapsed motionless again.

After staring intently at the dolls for a moment longer, Karen nodded at Bill.

"It's done," she said, laughing. "Mark and Becky are both gonna find each other irresistible now."

Karen wrapped the three carved figures up in the red cloth and replaced them in her bag. Then she gestured to her brother and the two of them walked over to their living room window and stared across the street at the Wilsons' residence.

"Poor Wendy," Bill said, after a mouthful of beer. "I almost feel sorry for her now."

"No you don't," Karen said, laughing and nudging him with her elbow.

"Yeah, you're damn right, I don't," Bill said, breaking into loud laughter.

CHAPTER 4

Yeah, honey-pie, we're still on for tonight and tomorrow. Wendy thinks I'll be attending a work meeting over in Phoenix.

Her heart full of pain, Wendy drove carefully through the darkness. Mark's bronze Toyota Camry was about a hundred yards ahead of her. Wendy had been tailing the car for ten minutes now. So that Mark didn't suspect he was being followed, she was keeping a cautious distance behind him, sometimes lagging behind in the distance while turned a corner, before speeding up to resume the pursuit.

It was nighttime and her own car was black in color anyway, but she wasn't taking any chances on him seeing her.

Wendy had never done this before—followed Mark to one of his many rendezvous with women—but tonight, she'd felt as if she had no choice.

She needed to see this for herself, to confirm with her own eyes the damning evidence she'd read in his cell phone's messaging app.

Mark had come home early this Friday evening and explained that in response to an emergency business call, he needed to drive out of town tonight to Phoenix so that he could be up early for a breakfast meeting with some potential investors.

Wendy had just known he was lying to her. And so, while he'd been bathing and whistling to himself she had decided to look through his phone correspondence.

Yeah, honey-pie, we're still on for tonight and tomorrow.

There was no mention of whom 'Honey-pie' was. The text simply listed her phone number, which Wendy had quickly copied down. But right there and then, as Mark had returned from the bathroom, grinning to himself and had resumed packing his bags for the weekend, Wendy had resolved to tail him when he left home tonight.

***

Since visiting her neighbor Karen yesterday afternoon, Wendy had had a sense of imminent disaster hovering over her. Although she had at first put her unease down to seeing all those horrible occult sculptures and paintings that Karen had all over her place (and also the strange hallucination she had had of her hostess changing into a giant black bird), she had finally realized that what was really upsetting her was how powerless she felt in the midst of what was currently happening to her.

She was easy pickings for the Devil. And even Karen seemed to have realized that much, tempting her with offers of supernatural power.

"God expects you to depend on him and then He disappoints you anyway," Karen had said with a mocking laugh while pouring her guest more coffee. "We of the Black Circle depend on no one but ourselves."

"But you get your powers from Hell—from Satan," Wendy had managed to argue. She'd felt that as a Christian she needed to defend God, even though she too felt He was letting he down. "There's always a price to pay for the Devil's gifts."

"And God doesn't charge you?" Karen said with a gentle smile. "What about all those offerings you give each Sunday? Listen, Wendy, let's face the facts. Imagine for a moment that our positions were reversed and I were in your shoes. How do you think *I* would handle Mark?"

"What do you mean?" Wendy had asked.

"We'll you're clearly not very happy with him at the moment. I can tell—your aura is miserable."

"I don't believe in auras," Wendy protested. "And I am happy. I'm very happy indeed."

"Listen to me," Karen had replied. "I don't mean either to pry, or to be offensive . . . but, you have the aura of a woman with an unfaithful husband." Before Wendy could argue against this, Karen smiled coolly and went on. "Okay, sorry, please forget I said that. But, let's assume for a few minutes that this is the actual situation of things for both of us—I mean, that we're both married to unfaithful husbands. You as a Christian have to weep and bear it, I assume. But how do you imagine that I—a witch—would handle such a situation?"

Wendy had felt trapped by the question. Then her eyes widened in shock. "You'd put a spell on him? That's it, isn't it? You'd hex your husband into remaining by your side?"

"Exactly," Karen said. "That's exactly what I would do." She gave her guest a gloating grin. "I wouldn't take that nonsense from him for an instant. And I assure you I would also teach his mistress a lesson she'd never forget." Then she'd laughed. "But, of course, this is merely a fictional scenario we're dealing with here. Just fantasy."

"Yes, of course it is," Wendy had quickly agreed. But the idea of magically chaining her husband to her side had really intrigued her. Why didn't Jesus give one the means to accomplish that?

***

Wendy slowed her car as Mark turned off into the parking lot of a restaurant. She parked about thirty yards from the parking lot turnoff and switched off her lights and waited. Mark was clearly here to have dinner with his mistress.

But Mark didn't get out of his car.

Wendy sat there, tapping her steering wheel in frustration for a while, then finally turning the car stereo on and tuning it to a local Gospel rock station. But then she turned the praise and worship music off again when she decided that God had failed her. Because if He hadn't failed her, she wouldn't be here right now, following this unfaithful man who kept breaking her heart.

She was still pondering this when a blue pickup truck drove past her and pulled into the restaurant's parking lot and parked on the far side of Mark's car.

Hey, I know this car! Wendy thought, a sinking feeling starting in the pit of her belly. And her worst fears were confirmed a moment later when Becky Lowe got out of the pickup truck (Wendy would recognize that red hair anywhere!) and walked round its hood to greet Mark, who'd now alighted too.

And then Becky and Mark were kissing out in the parking lot, and Wendy sat there, her fingers clenched tight on the steering wheel, feeling like she's been shot in the heart.

Oh, my dear Jesus! Jesus, Jesus, please help me! Oh, God, please stop this, don't let this happen to me again!

But she heard nothing from God, other than possibly a quiet voice telling her to remain calm; and reminding her that 'all things work together for good to them that love God.'

But Wendy was beyond the point of remaining calm.

She sat there and watched her husband and his latest mistress break their clasp and get back into their individual cars, and then drive out of the parking lot with Becky following Mark as he turned left onto the road toward Phoenix, where he was supposedly having his breakfast meeting tomorrow. Both cars rolled off down the highway and were soon out of sight.

But now that Wendy had confirmed what she'd feared, she no longer had any desire to follow them. What would doing so result in? Making a scene? At the moment Wendy felt too tired to make a scene. She felt too wounded, too hurt.

But, more problematic, Wendy also felt her Christian convictions—that complete faith in God which she'd had for the past fifteen years—slipping away from her. She felt as if she'd been cracked and the Christianity and infilling with the Holy Spirit had been emptied out of her.

And at that moment, a kind of darkness flowed into Wendy Wilson's soul.

She smiled at the dark highway ahead of her, along which her husband and his mistress had recently driven. "I think it's time I take matters into my own hands," she said softly. "If God won't help me, then I think I'm gonna start helping myself."

CHAPTER 5

Karen pretended to be surprised to see Wendy at her doorstep early the next morning.

In actuality she'd expected her the previous night. Through the eyes of a bird familiar, she and Bill had watched Wendy follow her erring husband to his meeting with Becky. The bird had sat on a windowsill and let them see Wendy's misery and the sudden grim line of determination on her lips that informed them that she had made a decision to do something about her situation.

And now Wendy was here. And she looked as if she'd spent the entirety of the past night crying.

Karen lost no time in letting her in. Enough time had been wasted already.

Nor did Wendy waste any time either in letting Karen know why she'd come over this morning. "I want what you're selling," she informed Karen in a flat voice once they were both in the living room. "I don't care what it costs me."

Karen gestured to a chair. "Let's talk about costs later. Of course, nothing's for free, but it's nothing you can't afford to lose."

"How about your brother?" Wendy asked in a worried voice. "His car is parked in the driveway. Won't he? . . . I mean, does he . . . ?"

Karen laughed. "Oh, don't worry about Bill. He's more into this devil-worship stuff than I am. In fact he got me into it."

"Oh," Wendy said. "I didn't know that." But that seemed to calm her worries.

Then, faking concern, Karen asked: "But what happened to change your mind? Two days ago you were a perky and happy Christian, inviting me to church and all that. And now, you look like someone beat all the stuffing out of you with a softball bat. What the hell happened to you?"

"It's Mark, that bastard," Wendy began, and then she spilled out the whole miserable story of her husband's continual infidelities. Karen was surprised. Yes, she had known that Wendy was unhappy, but not that she was *this* unhappy.

"And all that time we were both in church!" Wendy finished, with tears now running down her cheeks. "I really think God hates me!"

"Well, that's over now," Karen said. "If God won't look after His own, the Black Circle will."

Bill walked out of the rear hallway then, barefoot and dressed in denim shorts and a sleeveless tee shirt that showed off his many tattoos. He waved at Wendy, "Hi!" and then he walked through the living room and into the kitchen.

"I want the kind of power that you have," Wendy told Karen in an intense voice that was full of emotion. "I want the power to adjust my destiny as I see fit. I'm tired of being a victim and a sacrificial lamb. I want the power to . . ."

Karen laughed. "And to get this power, are you prepared to renounce and denounce the false god that you've been serving all this while?"

Wendy looked pained and uncertain. "Do I have to? I can't lie and say that I no longer believe He exists, but . . ."

"Belief isn't what counts here," Bill said, emerging from the kitchen then. "What counts here is allegiance. This is a war we're all involved in; it's all a question of which side of the conflict you're on." Then he paused and gestured back at the kitchen. "Hey, I'm making coffee. Do either of you ladies want some?"

Wendy shook her head, but Karen nodded. "Yeah, I'll have me some."

"Okay," Bill said, then he fixed Wendy with a steely gaze. "But back to what I was just sayin', Mrs. Wilson. See, we're talking here about the age-old war between Light and Darkness, with both sides claiming they represent the former and that their opponents are the latter. Do you understand me?"

Wendy fidgeted her fingers in her lap and nodded.

"Good. So what I mean is, it don't really matter which side of the conflict you're on as much as it matters that you're committed to that side. You get that too?"

Wendy nodded again and Bill went on: "So . . . all the powers and abilities you want—the power to remake the world to suit yourself—this you can have. But before you get them, you first of all need to renounce both God and Jesus. It's merely a technical thing, but we can't help you otherwise."

"Let me take over from here," Karen told her brother, who nodded and walked back to the kitchen. Once he was gone, Karen struck like a snake. Wendy was clearly ready to bite the bait; her reticence now was merely the result of her many years of Christian conditioning. "So, Wendy, you do understand what Bill was talking about, right? We're not evil people. And you'll soon be one of us too. But first . . ." she stopped speaking and looked expectantly at her female guest. This was the crucial part. One couldn't be forced to renounce the Christian faith. It had to be a willing act.

"I completely renounce Jesus and God!" Wendy said loudly.

"Repeat it!" Karen said in delight. "Repeat, let all of Hell hear you say it!"

"I completely renounce God and Jesus! Wendy repeated, a dark fire in her previously tragic eyes. "I've been a Christian for the last fifteen years and what do I have to show for it? Nothing but misery and a man who's doing his daily best to drive me crazy." She looked fiercely at Karen. "So yes, I'll scream it to the highest heavens if you like. I renounce both God and Jesus Christ!"

"Excellent," Karen said. "And now, Wendy, the chambers of the darkest powers of the air shall be opened to you."

"Yeah, Mrs. Wilson, welcome to the Black Circle," Bill said, reemerging then from the kitchen with two mugs of steaming coffee, one of which he handed to his sister. Then he sat down beside Karen and crossed his legs. "And I assure you, that from now on, the sort of supernatural abilities you're gonna have are gonna be out of this world."

Wendy grinned broadly at this. "I can't wait," she told them both. I really can't wait."

Karen laughed. "Don't worry, this is gonna be everything you've ever wanted and more besides." Then, with her facial expression becoming just a bit more serious, she asked. "Hey, have you ever heard of a witch's familiar before?"

Wendy looked bemused for a few seconds, then she nodded. "Yeah, I think so. Aren't those those animals . . . like cats that follow witches around?"

Karen nodded. "Yeah, exactly. Now, Wendy darling, how would like to have one, one that did whatever you wanted it to?"

"Except that your familiar won't be a cat," Bill added. "It'll be a bird. A big black bird."

Karen was more than a little bit amused by the expression that came over Wendy's face when she snapped her fingers and the black bird appeared out of nowhere. The bird, which looked like a large and very nasty crow, flaps its wings in midair over the coffee table for a while, before finally settling down on the right arm of Wendy's armchair, an action which made Wendy scoot away from it, as if she was trying to pass her body through the rear of the chair.

"Don't be afraid of it," Karen told her, stretching out a hand and stroking the black bird. "This is your new best friend. It's both a sign of our dark lord's favor to you and the channel through which you will tap the dark powers you seek."

"Touch it," Bill encouraged Wendy.

Emboldened by his words, Wendy stretched out her hand and did so. At first there was nervousness in her eyes. But that look quickly gave way to one of delight. Soon she was grinning as she stroked the bird and giggling like a little girl.

"That is the power of Satan you are feeling," Karen said. "Feels good, doesn't it?"

"I feel great," Wendy agreed. "I feel as if I've just been plugged into a generator!" The black bird had meanwhile shifted its location to sit in her lap, where, her eyes slightly glazed over as if she was under the influence of a narcotic, she now stroked it with both hands and cooed lovingly to it.

Then, with a new and dark confidence in her voice, she asked Karen: "So how does this all work? Oh, my dear God, I feel so damn powerful now; as if I could pick up a truck with my bare hands."

Bill laughed coldly. "Lady, you don't know the half of it yet."

Still stroking her new dark pet, Wendy looked at him in surprise. "You mean I-I-I can lift a truck now?"

Karen laughed. "Wendy, darling, you've literally no idea what you're capable of doing now. Now, listen, here is how it works . . ."

Karen began speaking. Grinning, Wendy leaned forward, eager to hear what she was saying.

Karen gestured at the black bird seated in Wendy's lap, and which now seemed to have fallen asleep. "Well, the first thing you need to know, is that this bird—or rather I should say your familiar—will accompany you wherever you go. So keep in mind that it's always nearby, whether you notice it or not.

And also, others will *occasionally* be able to see it too. Now you need to understand that this black bird exists to fulfill your desires. What I mean by that is, that you control it, it doesn't control you. But still . . ."

CHAPTER 6

"Hi, sweetie," Mark Wilson cooed softly into his cellphone, once certain that his wife was busy in the kitchen. It was Monday evening and he'd gotten home early from work. The phone had run shortly after he and Wendy had finished dinner.

"I miss you, baby!" came Becky's breathless whisper. "I loved the time we spent together over the weekend and I can't wait to do it again."

"Me too," Mark told her. "But you know how things are. I need to be careful of Wendy finding out."

"Yeah, I know," Becky said. "I need to be careful of my dad too. He grilled me with all kinda questions as to what I'd been up to over the weekend. You'd think I was a teenager again and not a woman in her thirties. But it's okay. I'll . . ."

Listening to Becky professing her desire for him, Mark felt the usual thrill that accompanied all his affairs. The thrill that seemed to have died in his marriage. He looked across his living room, into the kitchen, where Becky was still occupied with loading up the dishwasher, and wondered where they'd gone wrong.

But maybe Becky and I didn't go wrong at all. Maybe, I'm just weak or a damned fool. God certainly doesn't like or even condone my current behavior. I'm sinning with this woman and yet . . .

And yet Mark felt he couldn't control himself. Yes, his wife Wendy was a nice and loving and God-fearing woman; but she simply wasn't exciting anymore. They went to church together and prayed together, and did all the other things that Christian couples were supposed to do—he supported her and she supported him—but Mark kept feeling like he wanted more out of life. And that more always seemed to come in the form of pretty young women he could sweet talk into bed with him.

"So, darling, when can I see you again?" Becky Lowe asked, her voice as excited as that of a teen on her first date. "I really can't wait!"

"Let me have a look at my schedule for—" Mark began, but then was silenced by a loud noise from the living room windows.

"Ca-ca-cccaw!"

Oh, not that damn bird again! he thought, looking over at the window and seeing the huge black bird perched outside on a low tree branch. The bird had been there last night when he'd returned from his weekend tryst with Becky and it didn't seem to plan on relocating.

"Ca-ca-ccaaw!" it went again, the raucous noise seeming to penetrate his skull and at the same time fill him with fear.

"What the hell is that horrible noise?" Becky Lowe asked.

"Some crazy bird that simply won't leave our house."

"Darling, it sounds like a crow; and a very angry one at that."

"It's much larger than a crow and uglier than sin," Mark said, staring in an inexplicable horror at the bird, which now seemed to be looking directly at him. The way the bird was looking at Mark, he got the feeling that it was eavesdropping on his phone conversation. He felt there was something unnatural, even 'evil' about its behavior, and under normal situations—had he not be committing adultery with his next door neighbor—he would have invoked the name of Jesus against any demonic forces acting against his home and family. But now he didn't dare.

"I haven't seen a bird like this one before," he told Becky. "And it makes the same raucous noise all night too. If it hasn't gone by the time I get back home from work tomorrow, I'm gonna have to do something about either trapping or killing it."

"No you won't kill it, honey," Wendy said from behind Mark, almost making him jump out of his armchair with fright. "Leave the poor birdie alone."

"Hey, I gotta go now. I'll talk to you later," Mark said quickly into his phone and cut the call. He hoped that Becky understood what had just happened and wouldn't try calling back.

He turned to face his wife. "Honey, you startled me," he said, trying to keep both his agitation and worry out of his voice. She'd come up behind him so silently that he had no idea how much of his phone conversation with Becky she had overheard.

"Who was that on the phone?" Wendy asked with a broad smile.

"My secretary," he lied. "I'm trying to get things at the office organized 'cos I may have to be out of town again this weekend." Then, seeing the angry look coming over his wife's face and not wanting to get into an argument with her, he changed the subject: "Wendy, what do you mean, I won't kill that"—he gestured outside the window, at the bird that still sat on the tree branch, and which now seemed to be crunching some large bug in its beak—"that horrible thing? It makes so much noise at night that we can't get any sleep."

"I like it," Wendy said, walking past him to stand by the window, where she turned around to look at him again. "I really like the sound it makes—it doesn't keep me awake at all; it helps me sleep like a baby. And besides, the nice little birdie keeps me company in the daytime. You're hardly ever here nowadays."

Mark felt like protesting, but what could he say? Her accusation was right; he hardly was around nowadays. And he'd just subtly told her that he wouldn't be around next weekend either.

Oh, God, please help me! he thought. *Truly the spirit is willing but the flesh is weak!*

Wendy was still standing by the window. She'd now returned her attention outside the house.

Mark looked past her, at the black bird sitting on the tree branch. The horrible creature was no longer looking at him. Now its attention seemed focused on his wife. Almost as if they were having a conversation.

After a while the bird cawed loudly again. Mark had no idea why he suddenly felt so scared.

CHAPTER 7

Wendy waved as Mark drove out of their driveway. He made a left turn, waved back at her and then sped off.

Once he was out of sight, Wendy stepped out onto the front porch and then descended the porch steps until she could clearly see the pale blue pickup truck parked next door, in front of the Lowe residence.

Timothy Lowe, handyman and gardener at the Joy of Life Bible Church and Becky's father, was just exiting his front door, about to set off for work. The church was up at the end of their street, within easy walking distance and old Timothy never drove there; nor did Wendy and Mark on Sundays, except they were going somewhere else after the church service.

Wendy waved to the old man as he walked down his driveway. "Have a nice day, Mr. Lowe!"

"And you too, Wendy!"

Then when he too was gone, she looked up into the branches of the tree in front of the house and snapped her fingers. Like magic, her black bird familiar appeared on one of the lower branches. The bird had been there all the while, but had concealed itself from human eyes.

Now Wendy smiled at it, and she got a thrill from knowing that it both heard and understood her, and that it would do whatever she told it to. "Okay, bird," she told it, "let's see how good you actually are. Now, I want you to go over to . . ."

The bird flew off to carry out her instructions. Wendy watched it for a few moments and then returned indoor to vacuum clean the house.

***

Twenty minutes later, Becky Lowe left home for work at Wickenburg High School where she taught history. While reversing her father's blue pickup truck out into the road she glanced over at the Wilson's residence.

She sighed on seeing that Mark had already left for work. As she drove past the Wilson's place, she saw Wendy Wilson staring out at her through one of her front windows. Beck suddenly felt very frightened. Wendy had had a broad smile on her face and Becky could have sworn that the smile was directed at her. She had felt immense malice and evil radiating from Wendy.

No, you just feel guilty, that's all, she told herself as she pulled away from the Wilsons'. *You're imagining that she knows how you're hurting her.*

But Becky's guilt didn't really matter to her. She had no idea how she'd fallen for Mark Wilson. True, he was a very handsome man, but she'd never been interested in married men. Adultery wasn't her style at all.

But somehow, about a week ago she'd suddenly begun feeling a burning desire for Mark Wilson.

I don't know if I love him; but I know that I want him more than I've wanted anyone in a long long while.

Of course, Mark's wife Wendy presented a lot of complications. But Becky was certain that given sufficient time, she'd be able to make Mark see the light; she'd be able to convince him to leave his wife for her.

Of course dad's gonna make a huge fuss about that. It'll be a huge embarrassment for him since Mark attends the same church as dad. Poor dad. He's already worried about the church's dwindling congregation as it is; and the scandal of me and Mark is certain to make it dwindle even further. But then Becky's lips set in a grim line. *But I've never really seen the point of all his religion anyway.*

While thinking this, Becky had turned the pickup onto Vulture Mine Road. Now she could see the high school down at the end of the road, just past the traffic lights. Soon she'd be surrounded by the hustle and bustle of teens preparing for exams and have no time to think about her new lover at all. But for the moment, she luxuriated in sweet thoughts of the time that they'd spent together, of the sweetness of his kisses. Oh, she couldn't get enough of him.

Yes, I don't want to be a bitch, but Mark is mine now . . . and that means Wendy has to get out of . . .

And then she felt a horrendous pain in her right ankle.

She was just arriving at the traffic lights before the school. The lights were red and she'd been slowing down to be first in the queue of stopped cars. But now, even before she realized what she'd done, the pain in her ankle made her stomp hard on the accelerator pedal, making her car shoot forward into the intersection.

She looked down at her foot and gasped in surprise and fear; a large black bird was down in the foot well and was pecking at her ankle, its beak already red with her blood.

Horrified, Becky heard blaring car horns and looked up again. As she did so the bird apparently pecked her ankle again, because another sharp jolt of agony once more made her stomp on the gas pedal.

Oh, my God, no! Becky thought in terror as a white delivery van bore down on her, the driver seemingly unable to stop it.

She did her best to swerve away from a collision, but her pickup truck was impossible to control now. And then completely out of the blue, just when she thought she was out of danger, another huge black bird hit her windshield, shattering it so that she could no longer see the road ahead of her.

The next moment, the van in the cross lane slammed into the side of her pickup truck.

When Becky revived, she was being cut out of the wreckage of her dad's pickup truck. Sirens and flashing lights were all around her, as well as uniformed men and women speaking in concerned voices. Her head hurt badly and her chest felt like a heavy weight was pressing down on it.

But worst of all, as the worried paramedics pulled her from the mangled car and laid her out on a stretcher, Becky realized that she couldn't feel her legs anymore. Her body was filled with painful sensation from her head to her belly, and then below that point all feeling abruptly ended.

Oh, my God, no! Becky Lowe thought with tears spilling from her eyes, as she realized that she was now paralyzed from the waist downwards.

***

Hahaha! Yes, it worked, Wendy thought in delight. Becky was a popular teacher and the news of her car accident had quickly spread through the neighborhood.

Her husband Mark had been the one who'd given her the wonderful news. He'd video-called her to relay it and she'd been thrilled by the horror and misery on his face. But of course, she'd been careful to look sympathetic and not let him see how pleased she was by what had happened to his silly mistress.

Well, to hell with her. I hope she never walks again. That'll teach her to leave my husband alone.

Wendy felt beside herself with joy. She stared out of her window at the black bird, which was once more seated on its favored branch, its dark beak now stained red.

Her cellphone rang. It was Karen Houston.

Karen laughed over the line. "I just wanna congratulate you on Becky's misfortune," she said quietly. "So, are you convinced now of the efficacy of black magic. Does it compare favorably to Christianity?"

"It's much better than all that Bible reading and prayer," Wendy replied without hesitation. "And a whole lot quicker too. This sort of power is what I've always wanted, not the sort where I need to beg God Almighty and Jesus to do even the littlest things for me; and even that takes forever to happen."

"Don't kid yourself that God ever answered you," Karen said in a mocking voice. "I'm certain that if you carefully analyze all those instances when you thought you'd gotten an answer to prayer, you'll discover they were all coincidences." She laughed. "Yes, *everything* was . . . but of course, back then you were so brainwashed that you attributed every result of natural causes to God's work in your life."

Wendy considered that. She didn't know if Karen was right or not, but she was making an interesting point.

"And now," Karen said. "You're in the position to control your life. I doubt that Mark will ever stray from your side again."

Wendy laughed at that. "But . . . but, Karen, you haven't yet told me what payment will be required of me. You've done what I want, and I want to fulfill my end of the bargain too."

"All in good time," Karen quickly replied. "Don't worry about it. But first of all, there is something you must do."

"Yeah, what?"

"Well, now that you understand how your powers work, it's time for you to *really* begin using them. The Black Circle wants you to start sabotaging the Joy of Life Bible Church. Are you willing to do this for us?"

"Of course. I meant what I said when I renounced Jesus."

"Good. Now the first thing you need to do is join the church prayer group. And you must be constant at prayer meetings. Your bird familiar will accompany you to the church premises. Through it, Bill and I will channel demonic powers to disrupt everyone's prayers and cause confusion in the church."

"Hahaha!" Wendy said. "This sounds like it's really gonna be fun."

"Oh, yeah, it definitely will be," Karen agreed.

CHAPTER 8

There are times when faith in Jesus just don't seem to be enough. Lord Jesus, why on earth did you let something as horrible as this happen to my harmless little girl? And after I've been a faithful servant of yours for all these many years.

Such were Timothy Lowe's glum thoughts that Sunday afternoon, three weeks after his daughter's accident, while he walked home from the Joy of Life church in company of the church's pastor, Amos Fisher and the pastor's wife Madge.

Becky had come home from the hospital three days ago and Timothy was still scared to leave her in the house all by herself. Becky was so depressed now that he kept thinking she'd harm herself if she was out of his sight for longer than a few minutes.

Becky would never walk again; she'd be in a wheelchair for the rest of her life. The doctors said it was a freak accident because she'd been well cushioned during the crash by the pickup truck's airbags, but still somehow her backbone had snapped and sliced her spinal cord in two.

"After you, pastor," Timothy said and stepped aside so that the minister and his wife could walk along the driveway ahead of him.

Timothy considered his daughter's accident a double tragedy because she wasn't saved. Since receiving the doctors' verdict on her condition, Becky had been inconsolable. Had she been in Christ, Timothy could have comforted her from the Holy Bible, but now, when she stared glumly at the walls from her motorized wheelchair, he simply didn't know what to say to her.

What could he say? She'd been living in sin too at the time of her accident. That weekend when she'd borrowed his car and not come home, he'd known she was off to see a man. But even after the accident, Becky hadn't told him whom her lover was.

Timothy figured things might have been different if his wife Ellen were still alive, Becky might have confided in her mother about things like that, but Ellen had gone to be with the Lord ten years ago, and he and Becky had been living together ever since.

And so, not knowing what to tell his daughter to comfort her, he'd asked Pastor Fisher to come visit the girl and if possible speak to her about accepting Jesus as her Lord and personal savior.

"Hi, Mr. Lowe, how's Becky doin' today?"

Timothy turned back at the voice. It was the girl who lived opposite, Karen Houston. She was about his daughter's age—early thirties—darkly attractive but not a churchgoer either; one of those Goth sorts with lots of tattoos. Lived with her older brother, who seemed a rough sort.

Karen seemed nice enough though. Timothy liked her and now he waved back and replied, "Oh, she's doing better, I think."

Then he turned and hurried forward to join the pastor and his wife who'd ascended the front steps to the house and were waiting for him. Both husband and wife were tall, middle-aged, and pleasant-faced.

"I sense a deep spiritual oppression around here," Pastor Fisher said.

Timothy nodded and his glumness returned. "It's really strange, pastor, how things in this town keep getting worse for us Christians, isn't it? Like Evil never has an off day."

The pastor nodded. "True. But remember the words of the good book, brother Timothy: 'Many are the afflictions of the righteous, but the Lord delivers him from them all.'"

Timothy nodded, and opened the front door. "It's just that it seems so hard sometimes."

"I know, brother Timothy," the pastor said in a soothing voice as they stepped into the house.

"Hey, Becky, the pastor's here to see you!" She was getting used to the wheelchair now and could move around the house unaided. "Becky, Be—"

But they'd all seen her. Becky Lowe was near the kitchen door. She was slumped forward in her wheelchair, looking like she was about to fall forward out of it.

"Oh, God, no!" Timothy howled as they all ran over to her. Becky was still alive, but her eyes were shut and her breathing was very shallow.

But it was Pastor Fisher who saw the empty bottle of sleeping pills on the floor near the wheelchair and quickly made the connection.

"Call 911 quickly," he told Timothy. "And let's trust God that we're in time to save her."

***

"I feel really dumb now," Becky told her father and Pastor Fisher two days later, when she was out of intensive care and had been moved to a private hospital room. "But back then, killing myself seemed the simplest way to end my misery." She gestured down at her legs, which were invisible beneath the blue hospital blankets. "I seemed to have absolutely nothing to live for any longer."

And it really had seemed that way to Becky. All of a sudden, her life had seemed pointless. She'd lost everything and in more ways than one: Since her accident Mark had gotten back together with his wife again. The couple had come to visit her twice while she was in the hospital, but on both occasions Mark had hardly seemed to notice her. If Becky hadn't known better she'd have thought her ex-lover was under a spell. She'd caught his eyes and had seen no recognition in them of what they'd once shared. The knowledge had been crushing blow to her.

On the Sunday afternoon when she'd taken all those sleeping pills, she'd been miserably ruminating on how Mark wasn't even replying her texts or picking up her phone calls.

And that was when that horrible black bird had begun cawing outside the house. She hadn't seen it, but it reminded her of the insane hallucinations of bird attacks which had caused her accident (hallucinations, because afterwards she'd had no wounds on her legs and her windshield had been unbroken), and all of a sudden, killing herself and ending everything had seemed the most logical course of action to take.

And now . . . now, what she'd done seemed so stupid.

I'm going to fight through this, Becky told herself, and then burst into tears.

"Now, now, now, try to see the positive side of things," Pastor Fisher said.

That statement instantly stopped Becky's flow of tears. She stared at the pastor in some anger. "Look at me. What positives can you possibly see in my situation?"

The pastor smiled calmly and leaned forward slightly, so his fingers were resting on her right arm. "Becky, you're very lucky that you didn't succeed in killing yourself. You'd have gone right to Hell if you had."

Becky looked from the pastor to her father and then back at the pastor again. "For real?"

Pastor Fisher nodded seriously. "For real." Then he smiled again. "Now, young lady, you're in the Valley of Decision. I think you need to accept Jesus as your lord and personal savior. What do you say?"

Becky thought on it for a moment. Her father had been telling her for years that she needed Jesus, that she needed to be born again. And she'd always resisted handing her life over to God. But right at this very moment, she felt differently about it. She felt a quickening in her heart, the desire to experience this new birth that Christians always claimed made all the difference in one's life.

"Yes, I think I'd like that," Becky told the pastor, smiling at the two men beside her. "I think I'd like to become born again."

Pastor Fisher laughed. "Very good. Now, please repeat this prayer after me. . . . Dear Lord Jesus, I come to you now as a sinner I repent of my sins and ask that you cleanse me of them by your precious blood that you shed on the Cross of Calvary. I submit my life wholly to you and ask you to come into my life and be my Lord and savior. In Jesus' name, amen."

Becky repeated the prayer in quiet sincerity. And she found the result to astounding. All of a sudden, her anxieties and fears about the future vanished, and the darkness that had shrouded her soul and had made life seem unbearable to her for the past month was miraculously swallowed up in a feeling of lightness as if the sun had arisen at midnight in her heart.

Oh, my God, she thought in deep understanding. *God is real, and he loves me. I'm his daughter now. I'm a child of God!*

She opened her eyes and smiled at the pastor.

"How do you feel now, Becky?" he asked.

"Like my life just got restarted," she admitted honestly. "As if my past has been completely erased."

"Yes, my dear," her father said with a joyous smile. "That's what it means to be born again."

CHAPTER 9

Karen was incensed. "I can't believe how we've messed this up!" she told her brother in a rage. "The bitch was supposed to kill herself, not to find salvation in Jesus."

The siblings were viewing Becky Lowe's Christian conversion in a crystal ball. And now the image in the crystal ball turned murky and then vanished.

"Calm yourself," Bill told his sister. "She still lives just opposite us. She's within easy reach. What's important now for us is to concentrate on destroying the Joy of Life church."

Karen fumed for a few more seconds, then she got over her anger and smiled at her brother. "Yeah, you're right, Billy. We'll come back to little paraplegic Becky in good time."

CHAPTER 10

Wendy smiled and snuggled closer to Mark on the couch.

They were watching the detective show, *Law and Order*. Watching TV together was something they hadn't done in ages.

After one of the onscreen detectives captured a suspect, Mark bent down and kissed Wendy, which made her tingle with delight.

This is just great, she thought. *I've really gotten my old life and love back. I can't believe how much time I wasted playing 'good Christian wife' when there was so much dark power available to me if I'd just dared take it.*

It was her usage of this power which had also caused Mark to completely forget about Becky Lowe. Because Becky was still just an acolyte where controlling dark forces were concerned, Karen had helped her cast the necessary spell to purge Becky from her husband's memory. Otherwise she knew he'd be overcome with guilt and sympathy for the girl.

Wendy felt a moment's worry though. Karen still hadn't told her what price she was supposed to pay the Black Circle for their restoration of her marital bliss.

She keeps putting it off and . . . oh, I really don't know what they'll ask me to do. I just hope it's something simple, like causing more trouble in church.

Causing trouble in church had turned out to be easy. Wendy had done as instructed by Karen and Bill and joined the church prayer group. And since then the Tuesday and Friday night prayer meetings at the Joy of Life Bible Church had turned into a complete mess. With the power of the black bird augmenting her seemingly guileless suggestions, Wendy had been able to turn most of the intercessors against one another, until now there was more hatred than brotherly love in the prayer group.

There was so much ill-will between the church's intercessors that Wendy doubted God cared to listen to them anymore. And, just like Karen had pointed out to her, no one suspected in the least that Wendy was to blame for the current state of confusion.

If you ask me personally, I think I've wrecked the prayer group—nowadays all we do is argue about who should lead the meetings and what to pray about—but Bill and Wendy say to stay on there, that there's much more they want me to do there, although I honestly can't see what else I can accomplish there . . . so—

"You okay, honey?" Mark asked.

She leaned back and stared at him in surprise. "What?"

"You've got a preoccupied look on your face, that's all," Mark explained, then gestured at the television, which had now gone into a commercial break, with the screen displaying a Gecko ad. "You're not even watching the show. Are you sure you're okay?"

"Yes, darling," she quickly replied. "I'm fine. I'm just trying to work out tomorrow's shopping list in my head. Karen and I are going to the mall together and I still don't know if I wanna replace our bedroom drapes or not."

Mark smiled. "Oh, those. They still look okay to me. But whatever you say honey." Then he pointed outside. "Hey, your feathered friend is back again."

Wendy let her gaze follow Mark's pointing finger, and she saw her black familiar sitting on the windowsill with its beady black eyes intently focused on her. "Yeah, it is. I wonder what it wants this time."

"Huh?" Then Mark began laughing.

"What's so funny?"

"What you just said, honey: that you wonder what the bird wants now. That makes it sound as if the two of you actually talk to each other." He kissed her again and grinned as the commercial break ended and the cop drama resumed. "Anyway, don't worry yourself too much about the drapes. Buy whatever you . . ."

Wendy tuned him out and concentrated on the bird. Her asking what it wanted hadn't merely been a slip of tongue. She'd meant the question seriously; not that she'd expected Mark to understand that. Though not yet as versed as her tutors in communicating with her familiar, and unable to see through its eyes, if Wendy really tried, she could sometimes pick up the bird's thoughts.

" . . . Karen . . . tomorrow . . ."

Wendy really concentrated now, focusing on the bird's beady eyes, trying to peer into its little brain. There was more to the message that Karen merely reminding her of their trip to the mall. Slowly the words came to her:

". . . Black . . . Circle . . . what you'll pay . . . tomorrow . . . know the price . . ."

And then the contact was broken. The bird turned and flapped away from the window. Wendy slumped against Mark, who, thinking she was merely feeling romantic again, pulled her closer to him and kissed her hair. f

Wendy turned and hugged him tightly to herself. She felt very happy that they were once again living as a man and his wife should. She felt romantic, felt like making love with Mark tonight.

However, as she replayed the bird's message through her mind, she also felt very disturbed.

It's time, she realized. *Time to give back something in return for this wonderful happiness that the Black Circle has granted to me. Tomorrow they'll tell me what they want.*

CHAPTER 11

"Wow, we really shopped!" Wendy exclaimed as she and Karen offloaded Karen's purchases from the backseat of her car.

And really, they had bought a lot of stuff. They'd spent most of that Thursday afternoon and evening shopping. In addition to the bedroom drapes that Wendy wanted, she'd also splurged a very revealing silk shirt (at Karen's insistence) and some stylish pumps—that in addition to the week's purchase of groceries. Karen had bought lots of beer and not too much food. But she and Wendy had also spent about an hour in a shop in the mall that dealt in occult paraphernalia and Karen had wound up buying several books on magic, three ceremonial knives and an ornately carved mahogany box to keep them in. Wendy had balked at buying anything in the occult shop.

"Not yet," she'd told Karen. "Remember that I'm still a good 'Christian' woman. What's Mark going to think if he sees me studying books on magic."

"You're right!" Karen had laughed. "How's everything at home anyway?"

"Oh, great. I haven't been this happy in years."

"Oh, you she-devil! Are you keeping Mark away from praying and reading his Bible?"

Wendy laughed. "What do you think? I'm not letting anyone, God included, ruin what Satan has given me."

They were parked in Karen's driveway, behind Bill's car. With the amount of stuff that Karen had to offload, this was much easier for her than having to carry her purchases across the road. They hadn't been able to take Bill's car too because he'd needed it for some Black Circle business out of town.

Before walking into Karen's house with her latest burden of beer six-packs, Wendy glanced across the road at her own driveway. Mark was already home from work. Wendy loved that; it meant that he was looking forward to seeing her. She'd earlier called him at his office and asked him to buy something they could microwave for dinner as she and Karen had been delayed at the mall and she wouldn't back till late.

She returned her attention to her side of the road, looking up at Karen's roof. Two black birds sat up there, both of them identical to her own demonic familiar.

But as Wendy walked through Karen's bungalow to her kitchen, she grew worried again. So far today, Karen hadn't yet told her what the Black Circle wanted from her.

"Bill will let you know once he's back," was all Karen would say, adding, "but don't worry your head about it. It'll be something you'll handle easily."

Wendy had had to be content with that, but now, as Bill waved a greeting from in front of the TV while watching a program about handguns and violent crime, she found her apprehension increasing.

Finally they got all of Karen's things into the house and put away. Wendy made a quick phone call to Mark, telling him she was going to be delayed for a short while longer and instructing him on how to cook their frozen pizza in the microwave. Then she joined Karen on the couch and they both sat facing Bill.

Bill smiled at her, which was a change, because most times he was a very grim fellow.

"Karen tells me you're really growing in exercising your demonic powers," he said.

Wendy nodded nervously. "Yes, yes, but that's not . . . em, I mean, she said the Black Circle want me to prove myself to them. That I have to . . ."

Karen laughed. "Stop fidgeting. You're acting as if we're gonna ask you to stab yourself and spill blood . . . or to kill someone."

Wendy relaxed a little bit. "You're not? With all those knives you bought, I thought that perhaps . . ."

Bill laughed too. "No, Wendy, you don't need to cut yourself. Your immortal soul is now already pledged to Lucifer, what more do we need?"

This was becoming too much for Wendy's nerves. "So what then? What do you want me to do?"

Bill pursed his lips and, after placing his elbows on his thighs, steepled his fingers in front of his mouth. "Well, my sister's statement about not killing anyone wasn't one hundred percent accurate. You are gonna kill . . . I mean, character assassination."

Wendy looked at him in confusion. "Who? The pastor? But I don't really know him that well . . ."

"No, no, not Pastor Fisher," Karen quickly said. "Your target is Frank Everett, the head of the church intercessors."

"What you're gonna do," Bill said, "is you're gonna accuse Frank Everett of attempting to rape you."

"What?" It took a few seconds for the magnitude of the request to sink in and then she could only gape at her friends in horror. "Wha . . . ? You want me to accuse Frank of trying to rape me?"

Bill nodded. "Yeah. It's the perfect setup. In addition to being coordinator of the church's intercessors, Frank is also the church administrator. Discrediting him will be a double blow for our master Satan."

"But . . . but . . . but . . . !" Wendy sputtered.

"Relax," Karen said soothingly. "You're in no danger whatsoever. It's a foolproof setup. Tomorrow afternoon, call Frank and make an appointment—tell him you want to discuss your marriage—maybe, that you'd like some prayers about you and Mark's inability to have kids."

Bill nodded and took over from his sister: "Then you drive over to the church wearing something seductive and get Frank alone in his office. Shut the door behind you and come onto him strong, then rip your dress open . . ." To demonstrate, he made a gesture of pulling his hands outwards from the center of his chest.

Wendy listened with growing horror. *Accuse Frank Everett of raping me?* It was really too much to ask of her.

"No, no, no . . . I can't do this to Frank," she protested weakly. "In addition to Frank being a wonderful friend to Mark and I, his wife Nicole is a childhood friend of mine . . . we've known each other since kindergarten." She looked from Karen to Bill with pleading eyes. "Please, please, ask me to do something else . . . or to do *this* to someone else . . . If I accuse Frank of trying to rape me, it'll destroy him."

Bill laughed, got up from his seat and walked over to stand beside Wendy. She flinched when she felt his fingers on her head, stroking her hair. He'd never before touched her and now that he did, his touch filled her with revulsion.

"Destroying him is the entire point, Mrs. Wilson," he told Wendy, who looked now to Karen for support.

But Karen merely nodded back at her also. "Sorry, girl, but that's the way it's got to be. And remember, this is your payment to the Black Circle for your current marital happiness and magical powers." She shrugged. "Maybe, it'd be better if you viewed it this way; as a choice you need to make—either Frank goes down or you do."

"And remember where the Black Circle has lifted you up from," Bill said soothingly, leaving her side and walking back to take his seat again. "Remember how far you've been elevated, Mrs. Wilson. Barely a month ago, you were a depressed and almost neurotic wreck, wondering how you'd keep your marriage intact. And now?"

"Now you're free and powerful, and completely in control of your own destiny," Karen added with a mocking smile on her face. "And you're getting more versed in satanic rites daily. So you've really no choice." She paused for a moment, letting her words hang. "If you don't do what you're being instructed to and help us destroy Frank Everett's life and by so doing drive another nail deep into the coffin that is the Joy of Life church,the Black Circle will certainly take all your new powers and happiness away from you."

Bill nodded. "And you wouldn't want that now, would you? Not after you've renounced Jesus for good?"

"Oh, no no no, I definitely don't want that to happen," Wendy said immediately, a vision of her previous hopeless state flittering before her eyes. "I'd rather kill myself than be that weak and miserable person again." Then she stared at Bill again. "But this approach just seems so cruel and drastic."

Karen laughed loudly. "Honey, it's no worse than what you did when you put Becky Lowe in a wheelchair. And in this case, Frank even gets to keep his legs."

"Okay, I'll do it," Wendy said in a weak and miserable voice. "Just give me some time to think it through."

"There's nothing to think about," Bill said coldly. "The Circle requires that you do it tomorrow evening before the church prayer meeting commences. Either that or there'll be dire consequences for you. Very dire consequences."

Wendy gaped at them both. "Dire?"

Smiling coldly, brother and sister both nodded back at her.

***

Hell no, I'm not going to do that to Frank, Wendy thought in determination as she reversed her car out of Karen and Bill's driveway. *There has to be a way out of this mess. Oh, I definitely do love Satan now, not Jesus, but I don't see the need to ruin two of my closest friends simply to destroy the church. I'm sure that if can contact and discuss this with someone else in the Black Circle organization—someone higher up than Karen and Bill, they'll agree with me that we can wait until someone else whom I don't like is in charge of . . ."*

Thinking like this and concentrating on reversing and parking her car just right, Wendy paid little attention to her bird familiar as it flapped down from a nearby tree and landed on the hood of her car. The bird did this often nowadays, a kind of welcoming ritual which Wendy found ultra-cute.

Now however, because of her own preoccupations, she had no idea that the bird was reading her mind.

***

"Hi, honey, I'm back!" Wendy chirped brightly as she stepped into the house, her worries momentarily blown to the back burner by the smell of food coming from her kitchen. "Hey, honey, come and give me a hand with offloading the car!"

Mark stepped out of the kitchen and walked towards her with a broad smile on his face. "Hi, baby, I really missed you at—"

And, then just like that, Mark toppled over and hit the floor, where he lay gasping for breath.

"Oh, my God! Mark!" Wendy ran over to him and attempted to revive him. She rolled him over onto his back. "Honey, are you okay?"

But he clearly wasn't okay. He kept gasping for breath, and in addition his skin had begun turning an ugly shade of purple. A really nasty shade as if his veins were leaking blood under his skin.

"Help!" Mark moaned and then his eyes shut and the only signs of life remaining in him were the agonized rise and fall of his chest and his rasping exhalations of breath.

In a panic, Wendy leapt to her feet and began looking around for her cellphone. "God! Oh dear Jesus! I need an ambulance!"

"No you don't!" The icy words in her mind compelled her to silence. She looked around towards the window, where the black bird waited, gazing at her with steely eyes, but then she realized that while turning to look at it, she had seen something else.

Calmed for the moment, she turned back towards the kitchen.

On the wall beside the hallway entrance, large black words were forming and dissolving. The words seemed like a mixture of tar and feathers and a rancid stink of soul-evil came to her from them:

THIS IS MERELY A WARNING. WE ARE NOT JOKING WITH YOU. DO NOT BOTHER CALLING FOR AN AMBULANCE. IF YOU DO MARK WILL DIE BEFORE IT ARRIVES.

"Please, don't let him die," Wendy pleaded, addressing herself to the wall, where the word formed and dripped like black paint and faded.

HE WILL NOT DIE, SO LONG AS YOU DO WHAT WE HAVE ORDERED YOU TO. AT FIVE P.M. TOMORROW EVENING YOU WILL DRIVE TO THE JOY OF LIFE BIBLE CHURCH AND THERE YOU WILL ACCUSE FRANK EVERETT OF ATTEMTPING TO RAPE YOU. YOU WILL BE VERY CONVINCING IN YOUR CLAIMS AND YOU WILL STICK TO YOUR STORY NO MATTER WHAT ANYONE SAYS. THAT CHURCH MUST DIE, WENDY, IT MUST DIE!

Wendy nodded weakly. "Yes, yes, yes! I'll do whatever you say."

"GOOD! YOUR HUSBAND WILL REMAIN IN THIS CONDITION UNTIL OUR WILL IS DONE AND YOU HAVE PROVED YOUR LOYALTY TO US!"

The nauseating black words dripped and evaporated and suddenly the wall was clear again, the intense atmosphere of evil that had accompanied the words merely a memory.

Wendy knelt over Mark, whose skin was fully purple now—everywhere the color of a bruise. He seemed to be sleeping.

Wendy began weeping, then she got to her feet and scowled at the black bird which still sat on the window sill watching her.

Then she began laughing. "Okay, I'll do it," she said with determination. "Yes I will."

Her bird familiar nodded its head in agreement with her decision.

***

Wendy spent rest of that evening getting Mark set up comfortably in bed. She considered leaving him out in the living room, maybe moving him onto the couch and propping up his head with a few throw pillows, but there was always the chance of someone stopping by to visit her before the Black Circle removed their spell from him (including the police maybe driving her home after she'd accused Frank), and she'd have no idea how to answer the embarrassing questions that were certain to come from anyone seeing Mark in his current state.

Wendy utterly hated how Mark looked now, like a human eggplant. But once she'd gotten over her shock she also felt strangely pleased.

This is real power, she realized as she dragged him through the house to their guest bedroom, surprised at how Mark now seemed to weight so little, before she understood that her bird familiar was increasing her own physical strength so she could handle him with ease.

Once she'd tucked Mark into bed in their guest room—she wasn't sleeping next to him while he looked all swollen and purple like that—Wendy returned to her living room. She realized there was nothing else she could do for Mark at the moment— he seemed to be out cold. After sitting and pondering her next step for a few moments, she shrugged and walked outside to resume unloading her purchases from her car.

Looking across the street she noticed Karen staring at her through her parted living room drapes. She waved at her spiritual mentor and then got to work carrying her groceries into the house.

Tonight Wendy felt wonderfully calm. Tomorrow there would be hell to pay for poor Frank Everett.

CHAPTER 12

When Wendy Wilson drove into the compound of the Joy of Life Bible Church the next evening for her prearranged counselling appointment with Frank Everett, she had no doubts in her mind concerning what she was there to do.

Of course the first thing she'd done that morning was to call in sick at Mark's office on his behalf. She'd spun his work colleagues some vague tale of a sudden fever that had turned to retching overnight; and how this morning Mark had been unable to get out of bed.

Well, that last part's true at least, she thought while maneuvering the car through the parking lot. *At the moment, Mark really can't get out bed. And that's the reason why I'm here right now.*

She parked her car a short distance from the church building and sat behind the steering wheel for a short while to calm herself.

"How you doin', sister Wendy?"

Startled she turned to stare at the speaker. But it was just her neighbor Timothy Lowe. Dressed in his boots and work overalls, the old man was standing by her passenger side door, beside a wheelbarrow loaded with seedlings packed in bags of earth.

"How are you, sir?" Wendy asked, even though she wasn't pleased by the distraction and delay that a conversation with him would cause.

He smiled and, laying his arm on the passenger side windowsill, leaned into the car to talk to her. "Well, it's been a good day so far, praise God." He gestured back at the seedlings in his wheelbarrow, and Wendy now also noticed a pair of black trowels in there. "Just tryin' to beatify the Lord's house," he said.

Wendy forced a smile. "Oh, that's just great, brother Timothy. Hey, how's Becky doing? I'm sorry I haven't visited her for a while."

Timothy waved her apology away. "Oh, she's doing great, sister. Just great, thank God. Coming to our Lord and savior has really opened Becky's eyes to the fact that life has so much to offer her, even though she's now stuck in a wheelchair." Suddenly he looked sad. "I only wish she'd made her decision for Christ before her accident. I can't help but think that that car crash she suffered was divine punishment for some—"

"Ca-ca-cawww!"

"Oh, dear Lord Jesus!" Timothy groaned and grabbed his head.

"Are you okay, brother Timothy?" Wendy asked, hiding her smile.

Timothy Lowe groaned and turned to point at her bird familiar, which sat on a low tree branch and was staring at them both. "It's that damned bird, sister Wendy. Or, maybe one just like it."

Wendy feigned ignorance. "Yes, I think I've seen one or two of them in our neighborhood recently. "But what of it?"

Timothy Lowe looked back in at her and shook his old head as if to clear it. "I dunno, but they're a serious nuisance. I almost think the damned things are possessed. That noise they keep making . . . sometimes it's like a buzz saw drone in my mind." He sighed. "There's several of them that keeps hanging around my place and your house and the Houston's place. I just wish they wouldn't come to church too."

The black bird cawed loudly again, making Timothy Lowe grimace like he was in pain.

Wendy laughed. "Come on, brother Timothy, surely you don't think birds work for the Devil now? Whatever happened to demons?"

Timothy Lowe laughed too. "Yeah, you're right. I really shouldn't let them get to me. But that noise they make . . ." Then he shrugged. "But well, I'd better get back to work—these trees ain't gonna plant themselves." He gestured towards the church building. "You're a little early for tonight's prayer meeting ain't'cha?"

She nodded. "I'm here for private counselling with brother Frank."

Timothy Lowe nodded sagely. "Yeah, I hope Becky joins the prayer group soon. Be real good for her." Then he pulled his head out of the car window and picked up the handles of his wheelbarrow. "Okay, sister, gotta run. I'll be seeing ya."

She waved at the old man as he pushed away his wheelbarrow, feeling relieved when he vanished around the side of the house. Though their conversation had lasted less than five minutes, she didn't appreciate the delay.

She stepped out of her car and locked it up.

She stretched and then grinned at up her bird familiar, which flapped its dusky wings as if stretching too. She didn't feel worried. She felt like a soldier about to enter battle.

She'd dressed to seduce. In addition to high heels, she was wearing the tightest set of denim jeans she possessed. She also wasn't wearing a brassiere underneath her flimsy silk top, although this omission wouldn't be obvious to anyone because she'd draped a thick shawl over her shoulders, so she would seem chaste until she was alone with Frank Everett. She mused, thinking how appropriate that she picked up these attractive garments during her recent shopping trip with Karen. Lots of makeup and perfume completed her getup.

And then Frank'll never know what hit him, Wendy thought, licking her crimsoned lips, and feeling just a tinge of regret in her heart. *Poor, poor Frank. The rest of his life will be spent attempting to clear his name. In the heat of the matter, no one is going to bother asking me why I came for counselling dressed like a hooker.*

On the phone today, Karen had explained the plan in clear detail: "You just make your rape accusation against Frank. Once you've done that, we've several women outside the church who'll stand up to support your allegations against him, claiming that Mr. Everett also made improper advances towards them too."

"Just make it really convincing," Bill had added after Karen had handed him the phone. "Lots of tears

74

and hysterics and . . . Yeah, you gotta remember to rip up your blouse too, so wear something that'll tear easily . . ."

"But what about Mark? I don't want anything more to happen to him."

"Don't worry 'bout your husband. So long as you play ball with the Black Circle, nothing's gonna happen to him. Mark will be fine again by the time you get back home."

Giggling so hard now that it almost hurt her insides, Wendy strolled around the side of the church building towards the administrative block.

CHAPTER 13

Church administrator Frank Everett had been having a rough day.

Frank, a large and normally quite jovial fellow, was trying work out why the church's prayer group, which he was temporarily overseeing until someone else was appointed to head it on a permanent basis, had taken such a nosedive in the past month. Nowadays when the Joy of Life intercessors gathered for prayer Frank spent most of his time untangling the web of accusations and recrimination that had grown up since the last time they'd met, which meeting time had also been wasted settling petty quarrels.

Brother X was angry with sister Y; brother A thought brother B was trailed by a demonic spirit of lust. Sister C had seen a vision that Pastor Amos Fisher was erring from the direction in which God wanted to church to go. And so on and so forth.

So far Frank had had zero success in understanding why all this infighting had suddenly overtaken the prayer group. That this was an attack by the forces of darkness was clear enough, but to effectively fight the forces of darkness in such a case, one sometimes needed to be able to pinpoint the source of the problem.

"And now sister Wendy wants to see me too," Frank said aloud. "And though she claims that she needs counseling concerning her marriage, I'm sure all she really wants to see me for is that she's angry with something the pastor's wife has done, or because she doesn't think Mrs. Fisher is setting a moral enough example in her dress code for the younger women."

Frank sighed. A few more hours here and he could go home to rest.

Outside a bird cawed loudly. Frank looked out through his office window. It was another of those horrible black birds that seemed to infest the town of Wickenburg nowadays. Frank didn't know where the birds had migrated from—he'd never seen this species before—but he wished they'd just as soon depart for someplace else. There was something really irritating about the noise they made.

And at night too, they make such a racket that I can't sleep. And when I get up to pray, they make such a racket that I can't concentrate on what I'm praying about . . . !

And the distraction the birds caused him carried on into daytime. Like right now; Frank had been praying and trying to read his Bible, but had found himself completely unable to concentrate on the tasks. Each time that bird cawed it felt like someone was drilling a hole through his head.

He stared at the open Bible on his desk, then closed it in disgust. Maybe later.

The bird outside made its raucous noise again and then there was a knock on Frank's office door.

"Come in," Frank said, knowing it was Wendy Wilson.

The door opened and Wendy stepped inside.

"Hi, Frank," she greeted him in a soft and uncharacteristic voice.

Frank tried not to gape at her. Something was clearly off here. For one thing she was wearing way too much makeup. And her clothes were much too tight-fitting.

"Good to see you, Wendy," Frank said, indicating the free seat on the other side of his desk.

Wendy sat and pouted at him. "I'm sorry if I'm a few minutes late for our appointment," she said, then she suddenly looked miserable. "Mark has started doing it again, Frank. I don't know what I'm gonna do!"

Oh, God, no, Frank thought in alarm, with sudden understanding. *Please, Lord, don't let it be that her husband's resumed cheating on her again!*

With this in mind he leaned forward over his desk to comfort her, placing his hand over hers on the desktop.

"Everything's going to be alright, Wendy," he said soothingly. "Please try not to worry about it. Our Lord God is in control of your family situation."

"Oh, I don't know what I'm gonna do!" Wendy sobbed, leaning forward until he could no longer see her face. Her voice however, sounded weird, as if she was weeping and giggling at the same time. Frank began worrying that she might be having a nervous breakdown. As he got to his feet and stepped around the side of his desk to go to her, he felt like cursing her husband Mark for his philandering.

But they seemed real happy together in church last Sunday, so, when did this all start again?

But then, immediately Frank reached Wendy's side and laid a hand on her shoulder, she lifted her head again and flung her shawl away and leaned back in her chair. He gasped when he saw that she was practically naked now, her sheer silk top hardly concealing her body from him.

She came at him, rising to her feet and thrusting her breasts at him. And at the same time he looked into her eyes and saw a deep evil reflected in her gaze. "Do you like me, Frank?" she asked, licking her bright red lips. "I mean, like me as a woman? Wouldn't you like to make love to me here and right now?"

"Sweet Jesus, no!" Frank yelped as he scrambled away from her clutching fingers. "Calm down, Wendy." But she showed no signs of calming down and he began silently praying for God's help in this unprecedented situation.

And right then, it seemed as if a veil was lifted from Frank's eyes. One moment Wendy Wilson was leaning on the end of his desk and pouting her lips at him, and then next—as if he was dreaming—Wendy wasn't there anymore. In her place stood a giant black bird—a replica of the one outside that had been disturbing his concentration all afternoon.

"Come on, let's make love, honey!" the nauseating creature croaked at Frank. "I know you want to!"

Frank stared at the giant bird for a moment, and then just as abruptly as it had come, the horrible creature was gone again. And Wendy once more stood there by his desk with her hips cocked seductively.

"Come on, let's make love, honey," she pouted at him. "I know you want to!"

But Frank realized that God had just shown him a vision. He understood that at the moment, Wendy Wilson wasn't actually herself, but was being manipulated by a demonic spirit. And so, he did the scriptural thing and invoked the name of Jesus against her.

"You foul spirits of the air, I bind you right now in the name of Jesus. In the name of Jesus I take authority over every demonic bird spirit at work in my sister Wendy and I command you to cease your activities right now."

Wendy grinned at him. "Oh, Frank, darling you don't really mean that, do you?" Arms outstretched to embrace him, she took two steps towards him. "You want me too. You know you—"

"In the name of Jesus, keep away from me!" Frank yelled.

Then Wendy's face twisted up in pain and she slumped down to the floor and lay there twitching.

Frank looked down at Wendy, scared to touch her. The vision of the black bird was vivid in his mind.

Where on earth did she . . . ? How . . . ?

Wendy wasn't out cold. Her eyes were open and she was staring up at him as she lay there on her back. Her lips were moving, like she was trying to tell him something. Outside the office, Frank could hear a soft cawing, as if a bird was in pain somewhere. Looking out through his window, his earlier bird tormentor seemed to have vanished.

Wendy was still smiling seductively at him; she looked like she was still imploring him to make love to her. Meanwhile, though otherwise motionless, her fingers ceaselessly clawed at his office rug . . . as if they were bird's feet scratching in the dirt.

Frank decided that he couldn't handle this case of demonic possession on his own and ran off to fetch Pastor Fisher.

CHAPTER 14

"I don't believe this," Karen spat at her older brother. "How on earth could this happen?"

"Dammit, dammit, dammit!" Bill Houston was even angrier than his sister.

The pair of them had been monitoring Wendy through the eyes of a black bird perched up in a tree near Frank Everett's office. And now . . . suddenly the images the bird had projected into the air in the middle of their living room had begun wavering and fading.

"We need to do something fast," Bill said worriedly. "Before this situation degenerates further and our plans are revealed to the church."

The siblings hurried to make their quick and deadly preparations.

CHAPTER 15

"Oh, my dear God, brother Frank. Whatever did you do to her?"

This had been Pastor Fisher's shocked and worried enquiry on first seeing Wendy sprawled out and gasping on Frank Everett's office floor.

Frank had stared at the pastor in surprise. "Do to her? I didn't do anything. Like I told you, sir, she began acting all funny during counselling and I simply rebuked the demons troubling her."

The pastor nodded. "Okay, okay. Hurry up and fetch brother Timothy and let's carry her out into the main auditorium. She looks like she's having a seizure. Maybe we should just call an ambulance." Then he shook his head. "No, no, forget the doctors. This is a clear case of demonic possession."

Frank scowled as he ran off again to find Timothy Lowe.

Frank Everett had never really approved of Pastor Fisher's way of handling cases of demonic possession. He would have preferred to have had some of his other intercessors present, brothers and sisters who believed more in the efficacy of the name of Jesus in cases like this one. But the prayer meeting wasn't due to start for another thirty minutes and none of the church intercessors had yet arrived.

And even if they did show up now, there's a high chance that they'd be so caught up in malice against each other that they would simply hinder our attempts to deliver sister Wendy.

Once Frank located Timothy Lowe, the three men carried Wendy Wilson into the main church auditorium.

"What on earth happened to her in your office, brother Frank?" Timothy also asked as they bore their twitching female burden, who was now jerking like she was having a fit.

"She began acting all weird, so I simply rebuked her in the name of Jesus and she collapsed to the floor." Frank had decided he wouldn't say anything about Wendy's attempt to seduce him. Both she and her husband were very good friends of his and he didn't want to hurt their relationship.

The three men laid Wendy out before the altar in the front of the church, and then withdrew a short distance from her to discuss their next course of action.

"Maybe we should just call an ambulance," Timothy said. "This could lead to all sorts of complications."

Pastor Fisher shook his head. "No. According to brother Frank, she was fine until . . . please tell us what you saw, brother."

"While she was in my office, I saw a vision of a huge black bird," Frank told Timothy and the pastor. "Just like those ones that are everywhere now. It was shocking."

"Hmmm," the pastor said thoughtfully. Then he turned suddenly and pointed.

Frank and Timothy followed his pointing finger. Another black bird sat on a tree branch watching them.

"Although I think the bird association is purely incidental, we need to get to the root of this once and for all," the pastor said.

"Incidental?" Frank asked and then gestured back at the prone woman. "Sir, the vision I had was very vivid."

"Yes, I have no doubt that it was," the pastor replied with an assured nod of his head. "But while there is a clear demonic oppression at work here, both in this church and in this town, I believe the Lord showed you a bird merely as a symbol, an image of how pervasive the current oppression is. Remember that in the scripture the Devil is called 'the prince of the power of the air.' "

Frank doubted that this was the case, and looked at Timothy Lowe for his opinion.

The old man shrugged back. "I agree with the pastor. Besides, we can't go around shooting all the birds in town now, can we?"

"But come on now, we're wasting time. We need to get to the root of this," Pastor Fisher said." Gesturing to the others to follow him, he turned and hurried back over to Wendy's side.

Though unconvinced of the correctness of Pastor Fisher's interpretation of the vision he'd had, while following him back across the church, Frank was pleased to see that his wife Mary had arrived early for tonight's prayer meeting, along with another member of the prayer group, sister Juanita,. Both women were kneeling by Wendy's side with their lips moving in silent prayer.

"Lift her up and seat her on the pew," Pastor Fisher instructed Frank and Timothy.

"Are you sure of this, pastor?" Frank asked. "Shouldn't we cast the demon out of her first?"

Timothy Lowe and the two women nodded at his question.

Pastor Fisher shook his head solemnly. "Not yet," he said. "I feel this is a great opportunity to discover who is at the root of this. We will interrogate this demon as Jesus did in the case of the Madman of the Gadarenes."

No one opposed this line of reasoning. Frank and Timothy picked up Wendy and placed her on the front pew. For a moment she looked like she would topple over, but then she sat in place and stared at them with blank eyes.

"Tell me, you evil spirit, where do you come from?" Pastor Fisher asked. "Who sent you here and what is your mission in this church? In the name of Jesus I command you to speak!"

"Yes, speak, in the name of Jesus!" Frank seconded the pastor, while the others loudly chorused, "In Jesus' name!"

On this order, Wendy's dull demeanor immediately changed. She glared at them in anger. Her eyes turned black as night and her face turned bright red.

"I . . . I . . . I . . . I am . . ." she began defiantly.

But that was as far as she got. Suddenly a loud squawk came from outside the church, where the black bird had been perched, and Wendy instantly began gasping for breath. Her hand shot up to her throat as if she was chocking.

Then sister Juanita yelped in horror. "Pastor, pastor! The wall! The church wall!"

They all turned towards the wall she was gaping at. Between two windows on the church's east wall, giant black words were forming.

YOU HAVE NOT WON! WE WILL YET DEFEAT YOU! the writing proclaimed. Once formed, the words dripped down the wall like wet paint and then evaporated. Everyone stared at the wall speechless. No one even remembered Wendy, who was still gasping behind them on the pew.

"Who are you?" Frank asked, looking around to see if there was anyone in the church besides the six of them; but the building was empty. "What do you want with us?"

More dripping black words formed on the wall, and the writing seemed to stink of evil: WE OWN THIS TOWN! WICKENBURG IS RIGHTFULLY OURS AND WE WILL HAVE IT. WE WILL KILL AND DESTROY ALL OF YOU CHRISTIAN UPSTARTS. THIS IS YOUR ONLY WARNING!

"I rebuke you in the name of Jesus!" Pastor Fisher commanded. "Begone, you messengers of evil."

WE LEAVE YOU WITH THIS DEMONSTRATION OF OUR UNSTOPPABLE POWER!

Frank was suddenly reminded of Wendy again. This was because she gave a loud yelp of agony which made him and the others spin around to look at her.

But then everyone just gaped again. Though sister Juanita mouthed the name 'Jesus' repeatedly, her words were robbed of any potency by her confusion.

They all watched as Wendy's neck suddenly stretched out to much longer than normal, and then, while with terror in her eyes Wendy seemed to be trying to pull her head back down onto her body again, her head suddenly twisted all the way around to the back. After the resultant awful crack of shattering neck bones, Wendy's head spun slowly forward again and a stream of blood began dribbling from her mouth. The gleam of life in her eyes instantly began fading.

"Oh, my God, no!" Both Frank's wife Mary and sister Juanita began weeping.

Timothy Lowe stared opened-mouth at the dead woman, as did Pastor Fisher. Frank himself could only watch as Wendy's body, with blood now exiting her mouth in a thick red stream, slowly slid down off the front pew onto the floor again.

Frank did manage to once more look at the east wall. Now there were no evil words to be seen; that portion of the wall was as bare as before.

"Oh, my God," Pastor Fisher said finally in a tiny shocked voice. "Someone call an ambulance. Dial 911, somebody!"

Frank got out his cellphone and called Emergency. But there was clearly no hurry now. Wendy Wilson was dead.

CHAPTER 16

Mark Wilson was more scared than he had ever been before in his life.

Mark was floating in darkness, unable to either see a thing. He wasn't blind, but the darkness around him was too dense to see through. It had been this way seemingly forever now and he had no idea how he had arrived in this place, and when the mere torment of being here would end.

Mark had the clear idea that his being in this state now had a lot to do with Wendy.

All he could do was pray. He was completely immobilized, unable to move either his limbs or his mouth. But still, he prayed in his mind that God Almighty would forgive him his many sins. He prayed that God would forgive him for the nasty way that he had cheated on Wendy, hurting her for years and years with every willing woman who came his way.

If you get me out of this, Lord, I promise to dedicate my life to you again. And I'll treat Wendy like a queen from now on. I'll more than make up to her for every day that I've ever hurt her.

The darkness ebbed and flowed around him. And every sensation was pain.

Mark kept on praying however, hoping God still cared enough about him to deliver him from this place of seemingly endless torment.

And then a reply came: "I will deliver you, my son. I have done so already. But now, remember to always walk in the light of the word that I have given you." The word were quiet and pure and spoken with an unmistakable divine authority.

And just like that, it was over.

Mark opened his eyes and stared about him in confusion.

Where am I?

It took him a while to recognize that he was in the guest room of his own house. "How did I get in here?" he asked himself.

But he figured that that didn't really matter. He quickly got down on his knees beside the bed and prayed his prayer of gratitude:

"Oh, dear Lord Jesus, thank you for delivering me. Oh, Lord, I promise to live right for you from now on. No more womanizing. And, Lord, I really meant everything I said about my wife Wendy. From now on I'm gonna treat that woman just like a queen. I promise you that I will. I'll—"

Mark had to stop praying because out in the living room he could hear his cellphone ringing, and he realized it had been ringing since he'd come out of his 'daze' or whatever it was that had happened to him.

So he got up and went out to the living room and picked up the phone. He was a bit surprised to see that it was Pastor Amos Fisher calling him. He was even more surprised to hear what the Joy of Life church's pastor had to tell him:

"My wife Wendy . . . dead . . . died in church!? Oh, my God, no!"

Mark listened to what the pastor said; then he let the phone drop from his fingers and walked over to sit in the nearest armchair.

Then he wept and wept and wept. Wendy was dead now, and he had no way to make up for the horrible way that he'd once treated her.

The End

ABOUT THE AUTHOR

Gary Lee Vincent was born in Clarksburg, West Virginia and is an accomplished author, musician, actor, producer, director and entrepreneur. In 2010, his horror novel *Darkened Hills* was selected as 2010 Book of the Year winner by *Foreword Reviews Magazine* and became the pilot novel for *DARKENED - THE WEST VIRGINIA VAMPIRE SERIES*, that encompasses the novels *Darkened Hills, Darkened Hollows, Darkened Waters, Darkened Souls, Darkened Minds* and *Darkened Destinies.* He has also authored the bizarro thriller *Passageway,* a tribute to H.P. Lovecraft.

Gary co-authored the novel *Belly Timber* with John Russo, Solon Tsangaras, Dustin Kay and Ken Wallace, and co-authored the novel *Attack of the Melonheads* with Bob Gray and Solon Tsangaras.

As an actor, Gary has appeared in over seventy feature films and multiple television series, including *House of Cards*, *Mindhunter*, *The Walking Dead*, and *Stranger Things*.

As a director, Gary got his directorial debut with *A Promise to Astrid*. He has also directed the films *Desk Clerk*, *Dispatched*, *Midnight*, *Godsend*, and *Strange Friends*.

Also in Burning Bulb Publishing Christian Fantasy:

STRANGE
FRIENDS

GARY LEE VINCENT

PROVE YOUR
LOVE

THE BLACK CIRCLE CHRONICLES - BOOK 1

GARY LEE VINCENT

GODSEND

RICH BOTTLES JR.

Made in the USA
Columbia, SC
27 September 2022

67725029R00057